First published in the United States 1989 by Chronicle Books.
Copyright © 1987 by Ravensburger Buchverlag Otto Maier GmbH
All rights reserved.
Printed in Hong Kong.

10 9 8 7 6 5 4 3 2 1
Chronicle Books
275 Fifth Street
San Francisco, California 94103

Things I Can Make with
PAPER

Sabine Lohf

You can make all these things with paper.

Chronicle Books • San Francisco

Crumpled Paper Pictures

Animal Cards

Cut paper into strips.

Here comes
the wind!

Fold the strips in half.

You can use
these as place settings
at parties or send them to your
friends. You can even play games with
them. Line them up and then try to blow
them over with a straw. The person who
knocks down the most figures wins!

...raw animals on the cards.

Weavings

Stars and Snowflakes

1. Fold a paper square into a triangle.

2. Then fold it again.

3. Now cut notches along the edges.

Play Money

Place coins underneath a thin piece of paper, rub over them with a pencil and then cut out the coin shapes.

You can make a paper
coin wallet by folding a
square piece of paper
like this.

Silver Swans

You can make all kinds of animals out of foil. Decorate them with feathers and colored paper.

Can you fly?

Peekaboo Theater

Take a large envelope (or two pieces of
paper that have been glued together
along the edges). Cut out windows and
doors and slit openings along the sides
and bottom of the envelope. Now you
can slide figures like this in and out of
the stage.

Animal Racers

Cut out legs and fasten
them to the backs of
the paper animals.

Wow! Look
at them go!

Windmills

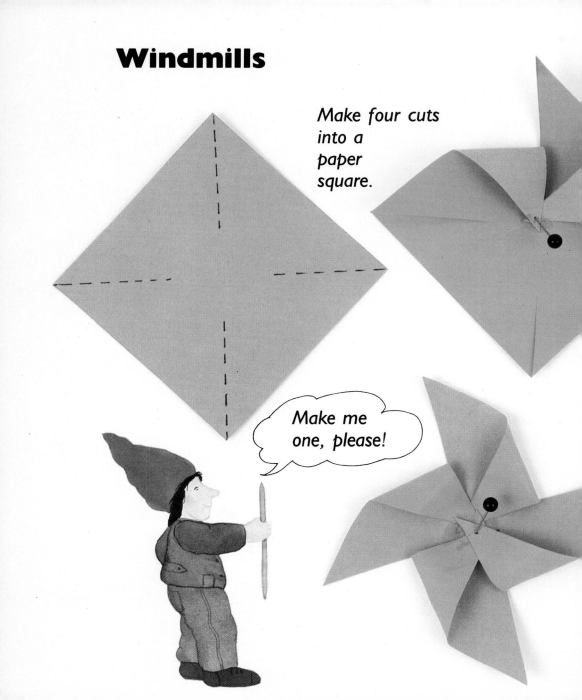

Make four cuts into a paper square.

Make me one, please!

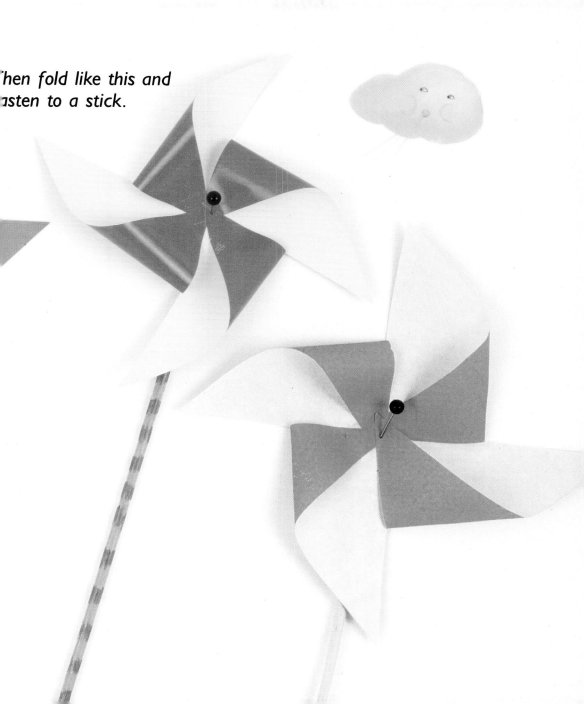

Then fold like this and
fasten to a stick.

Accordion Animals

Cross paper strips over one another like this, and then fold the strips alternately backwards and forwards.

Masks

Should we make a lion or a bear?